Sadie's Shabbat Stories

שלום

Written by **Melissa Stoller**   Illustrated by **Lisa Goldberg**

To Zoe, Jessie, and Maddie - May you always tell your own special stories.
And to Harry Zevi Berger, Samuel Berger, Reuben Stoller, and Jessie Mandel,
of blessed memory, thank you for sharing your stories. - M.S.

Dedicated with love to Natalie and Jim, and to the memory of
my Mom, Dad, and Aunt Viv, whose stories are always with me. - L.G.

Pronunciation Guide for Hebrew Words

Shabbat: sha-**baht**   **Shalom:** sha-**lowm**

Challah: **haa**-luh   **HaMotzi:** ha-**motzee**

Kiddush: ki-**dush**

Sadie's Shabbat Stories
Copyright ©2020 by Melissa Stoller
Artwork Copyright ©2020 by Lisa Goldberg
Edited and Art Directed by Mira Reisberg www.childrensbookacademy.com

Summary: Sadie loves listening to Nana's tales, especially about the traveling candlesticks, kiddush cup, and challah
cover they use every Friday night. Will Sadie ever be able to tell her own special Shabbat stories, just like Nana?
Based on true stories, this book celebrates family history and connections.

Clear Fork Publishing
P.O. Box 870 102 S. Swenson Stamford, Texas 79553 (325)773-5550 www.clearforkpublishing.com

Printed in the United States of America

ISBN - 978-1-950169-33-7

Every Shabbat, Sadie and Nana baked challah
together for the Friday night blessings.

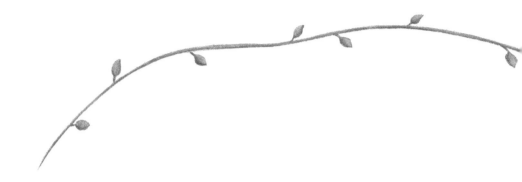

They set the table with silver candlesticks,
a sacred kiddush cup full of wine or grape juice,
and a challah cover to honor the special bread.

Every shabbat, Sadie asked Nana to tell her a story.
Sadie loved hearing Nana's stories, over and over.
Could *she* ever tell tales like Nana?

"Tell me about the candlesticks," said Sadie.

Nana pulled
Sadie close.

"The year was 1913. When Grandpa
was a little boy, he and his mother
visited his grandparents in Europe.

And then borders closed and they got stuck. For six long years, they couldn't return to New York. Finally, it was safe to leave. Great-grandma wrapped her mother's candlesticks in a tablecloth and packed them in a suitcase.

For weeks they rode by wagon, boat, and train. Great-grandpa waited patiently at the dock, arms wide open in welcome.

Now those traveling candlesticks hold our Shabbat candles."

Together, Nana and Sadie chanted
the blessing over the candles.

Sadie could almost imagine her ancestors
shimmering in the flickering flames.

"Nana, tell me the kiddush cup story."

Nana smoothed Sadie's hair and began.

"In 1916, your other Great-grandpa left his small town in Russia. It was a terrible time of pogroms against Jewish people.

Great-grandpa couldn't take much. Just his younger brother, some clothes, and this kiddush cup tucked into his coat pocket. America became his new home. This cup reminded him of family far away.

Now the traveling kiddush cup greets guests at our Shabbat table."

Sadie and Nana recited the *Kiddush*,
blessing the fruit of the vine.

Sadie could almost glimpse her ancestors
reflecting in the tangy grape juice.

"Tell me one more story,
about the challah cover."

Nana cradled Sadie's hand.

"My mother made this challah cover when I was a girl.

Her design of flowers, birds,
and Shalom - peace - hugged
our challah each week.

She presented it to Grandpa and me at our
wedding and we have used it ever since.

Now the traveling cover hugs our challah, too."

After the *HaMotzi* blessing over the bread,
Sadie and Nana tasted the challah.

Sadie could almost view her ancestors
weaving among the swirling cotton threads.

Sadie climbed into Nana's lap. "Here's a present, Nana.
A Star of David necklace I made. Just for you."
Nana placed the star close to her heart.

Sadie's eyes burned bright.
Images of her ancestors whirled through her mind.
An idea formed in her imagination.

"Nana, can I tell *you* a story?"

Nana's eyes crinkled.
"Tell me, Sadie."

Sadie hesitated. Could her story
be as wonderful as Nana's?

Sadie called up her courage
and began her own tale.

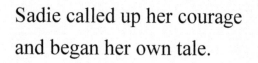

Sadie's Shabbat Story.

In Sadie's story, Sadie, Nana,
and their ancestors joined hands.
They invited the rest of the
family to sit together.
At a magical Shabbat meal.
With silver candlesticks,
a kiddush cup,
a challah cover,
and a Star of David necklace.

They danced the dance of

family, freedom, and peace.

Until the end of time.

Sadie told this story

and others.

Over and over.

Until . . .

Sadie's Shabbat stories
became as loved as Nana's.

And one day,
Sadie told these stories to her
own grandchildren . . .

. . . who wished they
could tell stories, just like Sadie.

Melissa always enjoyed hearing family stories and now she loves telling her own, over and over. She is the author of the chapter book *The Enchanted Snow Globe Collection: Return to Coney Island*, and the picture books *Scarlet's Magic Paintbrush* and *Ready, Set, GOrilla!* Melissa lives in New York City with her husband, three daughters, and one puppy, who all provide endless inspiration.

www.MelissaStoller.com

Lisa loves to draw and paint, and she loves stories that remind her of the magic to be found in everyday life. She often looked to Marc Chagall's dreamlike paintings for inspiration while creating the art for *Sadie's Shabbat Stories*. Lisa is also the illustrator of the picture book *Teddy*, written by Willie Devargas. She lives on the Lower East Side of New York City with her husband, daughter and two cats - just blocks from where her own grandparents lived when they first came to America.

www.LisaGoldbergIllustration.com

9 781950 169337